An **I Can Read** book

# OWL
# AT HOME

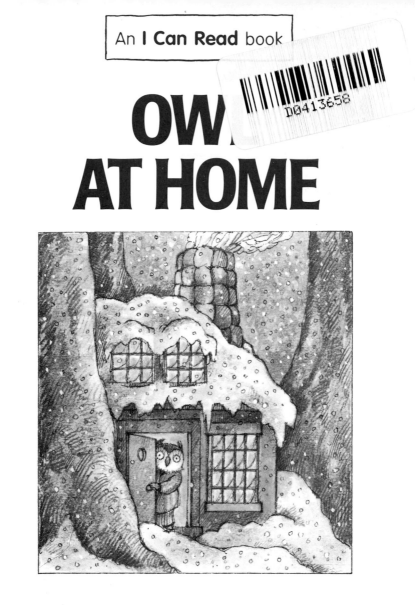

ARNOLD LOBEL

HEINEMANN · LONDON

For Grandma

William Heinemann Ltd
Michelin House
81 Fulham Road
London SW3 6RB

LONDON   MELBOURNE   AUCKLAND

First published in Great Britain in 1976 by World's Work Ltd.
Reprinted 1989 by William Heinemann Ltd.

Printed and bound in Great Britain by
William Clowes Limited, Beccles and London

This I Can Read book is available from
Heinemann Educational Books, Halley Court, Jordan Hill,
Oxford, OX2 8EJ, as part of I Can Read Pack 2.

ISBN 435 00071 3

# CONTENTS

# THE GUEST

Owl was at home.

"How good it feels

to be sitting

by this fire," said Owl.

"It is so cold

and snowy outside."

Owl was eating

buttered toast

and hot pea soup

for supper.

Owl heard a loud sound

at the front door.

"Who is out there,

banging and pounding

at my door

on a night like this?"

he said.

Owl opened the door.

No one was there.

Only the snow

and the wind.

Owl sat near the fire again.

There was another loud noise

at the door.

"Who can it be," said Owl,

"knocking and thumping

at my door on a night like this?"

Owl opened the door.

7

No one was there.

Only the snow

and the cold.

"The poor old winter

is knocking at my door,"

said Owl.

"Perhaps it wants to sit

by the fire.

Well, I will be kind

and let the winter come in."

Owl opened his door very wide.

"Come in, Winter,"

said Owl.

"Come in and warm yourself

for a while."

9

Winter came into the house.

It came in very fast.

A cold wind

pushed Owl against the wall.

10

Winter ran around the room.

It blew out the fire

in the fire-place.

The snow whirled

up the stairs

and whooshed down the hallway.

"Winter!" cried Owl.

"You are my guest.

This is no way to behave!"

But Winter did not listen.

It made the curtains

flap and shiver.

It turned the pea soup

into hard, green ice.

Winter went into all the rooms

of Owl's house.

Soon everything

was covered with snow.

"You must go, Winter!"

shouted Owl.

"Go away, right now!"

The wind blew

round and round.

Then Winter rushed out

and slammed the front door.

"Good-bye," called Owl,

"and do not come back!"

Owl made a new fire

in the fire-place.

The room became

warm again.

The snow melted away.

The hard, green ice

turned back

into soft pea soup.

Owl sat down in his chair

and quietly

finished his supper.

# STRANGE BUMPS

Owl was in bed.

"It is time

to blow out the candle

and go to sleep,"

he said with a yawn.

Then Owl saw two bumps

under the blanket

at the bottom of his bed.

"What can those strange bumps

be?" asked Owl.

Owl lifted up the blanket.

He looked down into the bed.

All he could see was darkness.

Owl tried to sleep,

but he could not.

20

"What if those

two strange bumps

grow bigger and bigger

while I am asleep?"

said Owl.

"That would not be pleasant."

Owl moved his right foot
up and down.

The bump on the right
moved up and down.

"One of those bumps
is moving!" said Owl.

Owl moved his left foot
up and down.

The bump
on the left
moved up and down.

"The other bump is moving!"
cried Owl.

Owl pulled

all of the covers

off his bed.

The bumps had gone.

All Owl could see

at the bottom of the bed

were his own two feet.

23

"But now I am cold,"

said Owl.

"I will cover myself

with the blankets again."

As soon as he did,

he saw the same two bumps.

"Those bumps are back!"

shouted Owl.

"Bumps, bumps, bumps!

I will never sleep tonight!"

Owl jumped

up and down

on top of his bed.

"Where are you?

What are you?" he cried.

With a crash and a bang

the bed came falling down.

27

Owl ran

down the stairs.

He sat in his chair

near the fire.

"I will let those two strange bumps

sit on my bed

all by themselves,"

said Owl.

"Let them grow

as big as they wish.

I will sleep right here

where I am safe."

28

And that is what he did.

# TEAR-WATER TEA

Owl took the kettle
out of the cupboard.
"Tonight I will make
tear-water tea," he said.
He put the kettle on his lap.
"Now," said Owl,
"I will begin."
Owl sat very still.
He began to think of
things that were sad.

"Chairs with broken legs,"

said Owl.

His eyes

began to water.

"Songs that cannot be sung,"

said Owl,

"because the words

have been forgotten."

Owl began to cry.

A large tear

rolled down

and dropped

into the kettle.

"Spoons that have fallen

behind the stove

and are never seen again,"

said Owl.

More tears dropped down

into the kettle.

33

"Books that cannot
be read," said Owl,
"because some of the pages
have been torn out."

"Clocks that have stopped,"
said Owl,
"with no one near
to wind them up."

Owl was crying.

Many large tears

dropped into the kettle.

"Mornings nobody saw

because everybody

was sleeping,"

sobbed Owl.

"Mashed potatoes
left on a plate," he cried,
"because no one
wanted to eat them.
And pencils
that are too short to use."

Owl thought about
many other sad things.
He cried and cried.

Soon the kettle

was all filled up

with tears.

"There," said Owl.

"That does it!"

Owl stopped crying.

He put the kettle

on the stove

to boil for tea.

Owl felt happy

as he filled his cup.

"It tastes

a little bit salty,"

he said,

"but tear-water tea

is always very good."

# UPSTAIRS AND DOWNSTAIRS

Owl's house had an upstairs

and a downstairs.

The staircase had

twenty steps.

Some of the time

Owl was upstairs

in his bedroom.

At other times

Owl was downstairs

in his living room.

When Owl was downstairs

he said, "I wonder

how my upstairs is?"

When Owl was upstairs

he said, "I wonder

how my downstairs

is doing?

I am always missing

one place or the other.

There must be a way," said Owl,

"to be upstairs

and to be downstairs

at the same time."

"Perhaps if I run
very very fast,
I can be
in both places at once."
Owl ran up
the stairs.
"I am up," he said.

Owl ran down the stairs.
"I am down,"
he said.

Owl ran

up and down

the stairs

faster and faster.

"Owl!" he cried.

"Are you downstairs?"

There was no answer.

"No," said Owl.

"I am not downstairs

because I am upstairs.

I am not running fast enough."

44

"Owl!" he shouted.

"Are you upstairs?"

There was no answer.

"No," said Owl.

"I am not upstairs

because I am downstairs.

I must run even faster."

"Faster, faster, faster!"

cried Owl.

Owl ran upstairs

and downstairs

all evening.

But he could not be

in both places at once.

"When I am up," said Owl,

"I am not down.

When I am down

I am not up.

All I am is very tired!"

Owl sat down to rest.

He sat on the tenth step

because it was a place

that was

right in the middle.

# OWL AND THE MOON

One night

Owl went down

to the seashore.

He sat on a large rock

and looked out at the waves.

Everything was dark.

Then a small tip

of the moon

came up

over the edge of the sea.

Owl watched the moon.

It climbed higher and higher

into the sky.

Soon the whole, round moon

was shining.

Owl sat on the rock

and looked up at the moon

for a long time.

"If I am looking

at you, moon,

then you must be

looking back at me.

We must be

very good friends."

The moon did not answer,

but Owl said,

"I will come back

and see you again, moon.

But now I must go home."

Owl walked down the path.

He looked up at the sky.

The moon was still there.

It was following him.

"No, no, moon," said Owl.

"It is kind of you

to light my way.

But you must stay up

over the sea

where you look so splendid."

Owl walked on a little farther.

He looked at the sky again.

There was the moon
still coming after him.
"Dear moon," said Owl,
"you really must not
come home with me.
My house is small.
You would not fit
through the door.
And I have nothing
to give you for supper."

Owl kept on walking.

The moon

sailed after him

over the tops of the trees.

"Moon," said Owl,

"I think that

you do not hear me."

Owl climbed

to the top of a hill.

He shouted

as loudly as he could,

"Good-bye, moon!"

The moon went behind some clouds.

Owl looked and looked.

The moon was gone.

"It is always

a little sad

to say good-bye to a friend,"

said Owl.

Owl came home.

He put on his pyjamas

and went to bed.

The room was very dark.

Owl was still feeling sad.

All at once,

Owl's bedroom

was filled with silver light.

Owl looked out of the window.

The moon was coming

from behind the clouds.

"Moon, you have followed me

all the way home.

What a good, round friend

you are!" said Owl.

Then Owl put his head

on the pillow

and closed his eyes.

The moon was shining

down through the window.

Owl did not

feel sad at all.